ASIA

AFRICA

PACIFIC
OCEAN

INDIAN
OCEAN

ATLANTIC
OCEAN

Thailand, where
Sunda pangolins like
Preeya and Chatri live.

AUSTRALIA

Where Pangolins Live in the World

Pangolins are some of the most unusual animals in the world—they are the only mammals with scales! Sadly, pangolins are quickly disappearing from our planet because they are illegally hunted and then sold for their meat and scales, which is called wildlife trafficking. But, if we work together, it's not too late to save them. My hope is that future generations will have the joy of living in a world where pangolins still exist.

~ Carrie Hasler, author

A Wish for Pangolin

was published by San Diego Zoo Global Press in
association with Blue Sneaker Press. Through these
publishing efforts, we seek to inspire multiple generations to
care about wildlife, the natural world, and conservation.

This book is dedicated to the people and organizations committed to
saving pangolins—our hope is that through more information, communication,
and conservation efforts, pangolins will no longer be endangered.

~ Carrie and Christina

San Diego Zoo Global is committed to leading the fight
against extinction. It saves species worldwide by uniting its
expertise in animal care and conservation science with its
dedication to inspire a passion for nature.

Paul Baribault, *President and Chief Executive Officer*
Shawn Dixon, *Chief Operating Officer*
Yvonne Miles, *Corporate Director of Retail*
Georgeanne Irvine, *Director of Corporate Publishing*

San Diego Zoo Global
P.O. Box 120551
San Diego, CA 92112-0551
sandiegozoo.org | 619-231-1515

San Diego Zoo Global's publishing partner is
Blue Sneaker Press, an imprint of
Southwestern Publishing House, Inc.,
2451 Atrium Way, Nashville, TN 37214.

Southwestern Publishing House is a wholly
owned subsidiary of Southwestern Family
of Companies, Nashville, Tennessee.

Southwestern Publishing House, Inc.
swpublishinghouse.com | 800-358-0560

Christopher G. Capen, *President*
Kristin Connelly, *Managing Editor*
Lori Sandstrom, *Art Director*

ISBN: 978-1-943198-11-5 | Library of Congress Control Number: 2019919688
Printed in the Republic of Korea | 10 9 8 7 6 5 4 3 2 1

A Wish for Pangolin

Written by Carrie Hasler

Illustrated by Christina Wald

SAN DIEGO ZOO GLOBAL PRESS

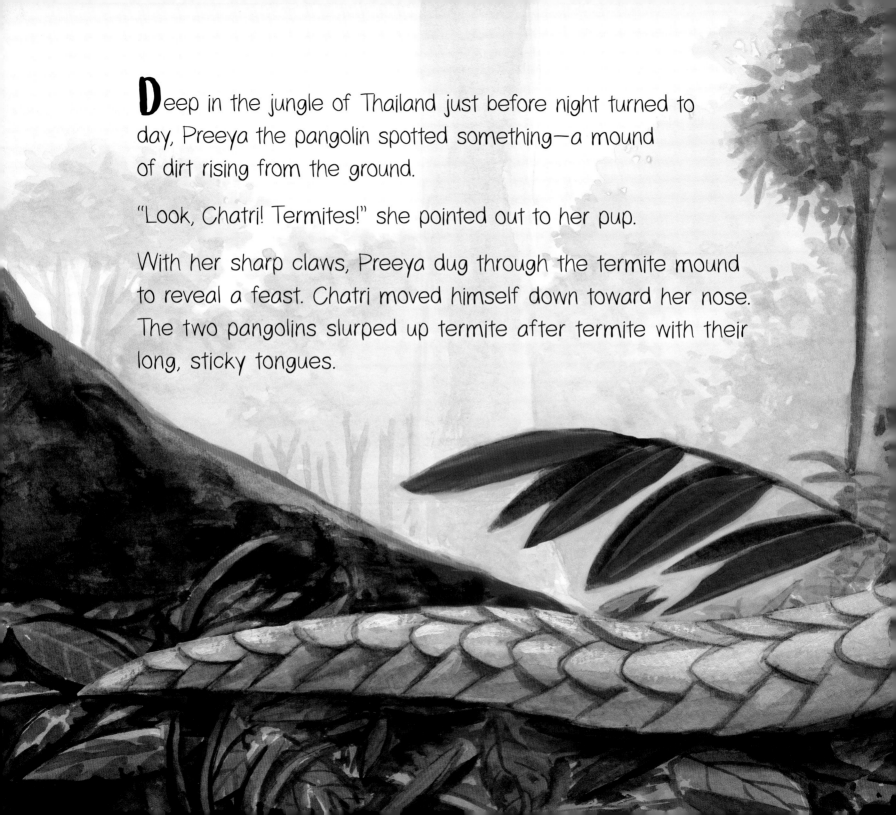

Deep in the jungle of Thailand just before night turned to day, Preeya the pangolin spotted something—a mound of dirt rising from the ground.

"Look, Chatri! Termites!" she pointed out to her pup.

With her sharp claws, Preeya dug through the termite mound to reveal a feast. Chatri moved himself down toward her nose. The two pangolins slurped up termite after termite with their long, sticky tongues.

As the pangolins ate, Preeya looked down.
She saw footprints. Human footprints.

"Chatri, it's not safe here. Hurry," Preeya called anxiously.

Chatri crawled up his mother's tail and clung to her back.

The pangolins quickly scurried to their fig tree home. Its
enormous roots spread across the jungle floor like tentacles.
Preeya began expertly climbing with Chatri riding piggyback.
High up in the tree, where a branch met the trunk, the
pangolins slipped into the safety of a hollow just as the
dawn was breaking.

"Mama, why did we have to hurry home?" Chatri asked.

"Those footprints belong to hunters," Preeya replied. "We need to hide. Plus, it's time for us to sleep."

"But why do we sleep during the day?"

"We pangolins are nocturnal," Preeya answered. "We're supposed to sleep during the day and find our food at night. But we have to be extra careful in the dark."

"So the hunters don't catch us?" Chatri asked.

"That's right. So the hunters don't catch us."

Preeya looked at Chatri. "See our scales?" She pointed at the hard, brown scales that covered both of their bodies. "They protect us."

"Like a shield?" Chatri asked.

"That's right. Like a shield," Preeya answered. "But they don't protect us from everything. They won't protect us from the hunters. We'll have to find a new home—one that's safe and far away from them."

Chatri looked worried. "Mama, I'm scared."

Preeya curled her tail around her pup.
"Chatri, did you know that your name means
'brave knight'? Your scales are like a coat of armor, just like
what a brave knight wears."

"You will have to be brave," Preeya continued. "I know you can do it."

Chatri looked down at his scales.

"Our scales make us look like an artichoke!" Chatri realized.

"Or a pinecone!" his mother smiled back.

"Or even a pineapple!" he replied.

Preeya and Chatri giggled. Comforted, Chatri curled up
with his mother and fell asleep.

Just as the bright light of the afternoon sun began to soften into dusk, the pangolins woke up. It was time to begin their search for a new home. With Chatri on her back, Preeya cautiously made her way along the forest floor, always on the lookout for more footprints. She used her strong sense of smell to detect human scent.

"Hold on tight, Chatri," she instructed, "and be very quiet."

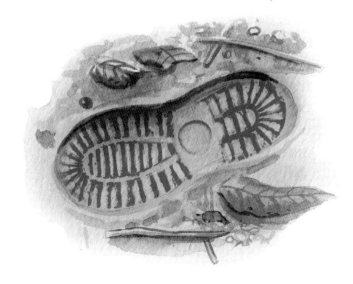

Deeper into the forest they went. Preeya saw fewer and fewer footprints. This must be the right direction, she thought. When they approached a clearing, Preeya paused.

"Look, Mama!" Chatri whispered. Together they looked up at the full moon, which hung in the sky like a pearl.

"It's beautiful," she replied. But a full moon would also make it easier for hunters to see them. "We must stay in the shadows, Chatri."

Through a thicket they could see a small herd of elephants huddled together.

"What are they doing?" Chatri asked.

"It looks like they are getting ready for the Lantern Festival," Preeya answered. "The elephants will light the lanterns and then release them into the night sky."

"But why?" Chatri asked.

"It's a time for letting go of worries. When the lanterns drift away, it's like the worries are drifting away with them," Preeya explained. "And then we get to make a wish."

Chatri smiled. He liked making wishes.

Suddenly, the pangolins heard a rustling in the leaves and brush. Something was approaching—hunters! In one swift move, Preeya turned over, hugged Chatri, and rolled into a tight ball around him.

Preeya could feel her heart pounding. She tightened her coil around Chatri. And Chatri made a wish—that his coat of armor would indeed make him a brave knight.

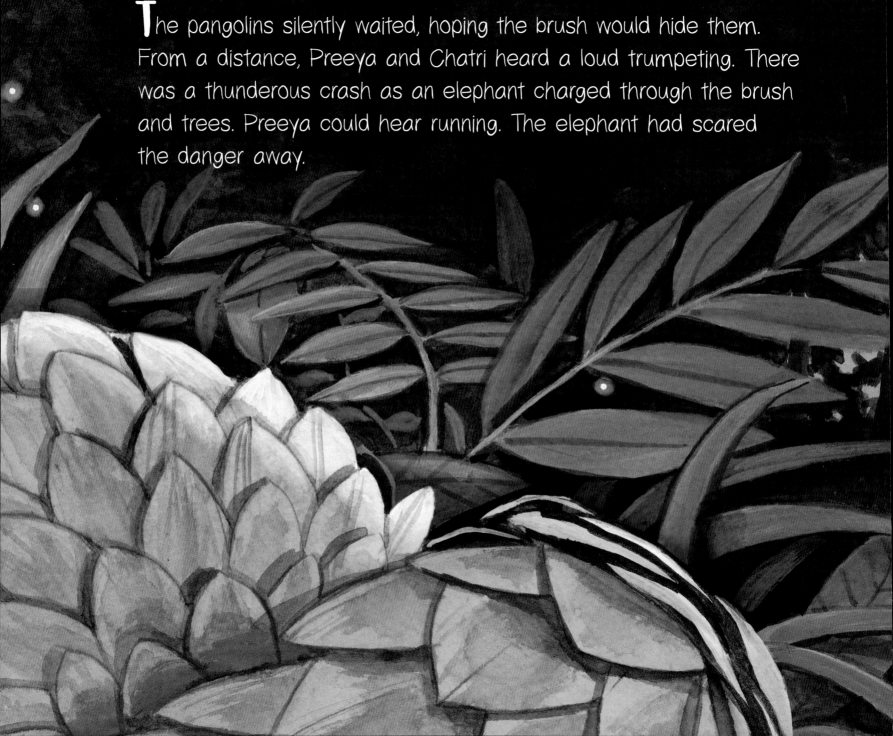

The pangolins silently waited, hoping the brush would hide them. From a distance, Preeya and Chatri heard a loud trumpeting. There was a thunderous crash as an elephant charged through the brush and trees. Preeya could hear running. The elephant had scared the danger away.

Before they knew it, Preeya and Chatri were swept up and carefully placed high on the safety of the elephant's back. Unrolling herself, Preeya nodded at the elephant.

"Thank you, my friend."

"You are very welcome," the elephant said with a smile. "I will take you to a new home high on the hill where the hunters cannot find you."

With her size and strength, the elephant easily carried the pangolin pair up the hillside. When they reached the bank of a swiftly flowing river, they stopped.

"The other side is very steep—too steep for the hunters," the elephant explained. "The gibbon will take you to the tallest tree. There is a hollow at the top where you will be safe."

On the other side of the river, a gibbon waited.

The elephant strode across the river and placed the pangolins on a branch of an impossibly tall tree. Together with the gibbon, they climbed up to the hollow. Filled with gratitude, Preeya thanked both the gibbon and the elephant who disappeared back into the lush forest.

Safe at last, Preeya and Chatri sat high on a branch where they could see across the whole forest.

"Mama, I see the lanterns!" Chatri announced. Like glowing jellyfish carried by ocean currents, the elephants' lanterns emerged from the clearing and floated above them in a beautiful sea of light. As the lanterns drifted into the sky, the pangolins could feel their hearts lighten, their worries carried away.

Preeya and Chatri snuggled together under the sky's magical glow. "Let's make a wish, Mama," said Chatri with a smile.

And together they did.

Fabian von Poser

Wildlife Reserves Singapore/David Tan Siah Hin

Our Wish:
PROTECT PANGOLINS!

All eight pangolin species are disappearing from the wild at an alarming rate. They are the most widely trafficked mammal on the planet! That means that poachers are illegally capturing and killing wild pangolins, and then selling them.

Some of the reasons for this include:

- People mistakenly believe that pangolin scales have healing powers or can guard against evil spirits. That's not true—their scales are made of keratin, the same material as our fingernails.

- Pangolin meat is considered a delicacy in some countries.

There is hope!

It's not too late to save the pangolins from disappearing forever:

- Scientists are studying pangolins and their habitats to find ways to help them survive.

- Rangers and wildlife authorities are being trained to stop hunters from poaching pangolins.

- Wildlife experts are learning how to treat and rehabilitate pangolins seized from illegal traders so they can be returned to their native habitats.

How You Can Help:

Learn how you can help San Diego Zoo Global
lead the fight against extinction by visiting:

endextinction.org
and
sandiegozookids.org/save-animals

• • •

Learn more about pangolins by visiting:

savepangolins.org

pangolincrisisfund.org

pangolinconservation.org

More Fun Facts!

Baby pangolins ride on the backs and tails of their mothers.

Pangolins can live up to 10 years in some zoos. It is unknown how long they can live in the wild.

Yi Peng is a lantern festival celebrated in Thailand to welcome the new year.

During Yi Peng, lanterns are released as symbols of worries and problems floating away. Wishes are made as the lanterns drift into the sky.

Some species, like the Sunda pangolin, have prehensile tails, which means they can use them to hang on to tree branches.

When threatened, pangolins roll up into a ball, using their scales like armor to protect themselves.

For protection, a mother will roll up around her baby, which also rolls into a ball.

Pangolins don't have scales on their undersides. Instead, their tummies are covered with sparse fur.